UNMASKING THE BILLIONAIRE

EMMA BRAY

CHAPTER 1

Eve

"I can't believe I let you talk me into this!" I practically have to yell over the music to be heard by Jenny, my best friend since childhood.

Jenny just smiles her dazzling, millionaire-dollar, rich girl smile at me from behind her sparkling, Swarovski-crystal mask.

We're at some sort of masquerade ball for New York's elite. It's the Halloween party of the season and surprisingly not as stuffy as I'd expected it to be.

Honestly, it's kind of cool with the dim lighting, high-end decorations, elaborate costumes, and all the masked faces on parade, but still.

This isn't my element.

"Oh, come on, Eve! This is fun! You need to lighten up and live a little for once!"

That's easy for her to say. She's a trust fund baby without a care in the world. Her mommy and daddy pay for everything, from her expensive haircut to the designer shoes on her feet. She doesn't have to worry about anything.

Not that I begrudge my bestie anything. I'm glad she hasn't had the same struggles in life I've had. It's how she's able to have that beautiful, happy glow about her.

She doesn't know the worry that I do of how she's going to pay next month's rent or how she's going to juggle the electric bill so that the power doesn't get cut off.

And while she's offered to pay my bills before or let me move in with her, I have way too much pride to accept her offers.

I've been making it on my own since I turned eighteen and aged out of the group home, and I'm not about to start accepting charity now that I'm twenty.

"Your birthday only comes around once a year!" she reminds me, flinging an arm around my shoulder familiarly. "It's time to turn up and party!" She pronounces "party" like "par-tay," and I can't help the smile that ghosts across my lips at her giddiness.

Jenny is a blonde bombshell. Model thin, tan, and tall, she's all bubbly and light whereas I almost look like a goth chick with my midnight black hair, pale complexion, and short stature. And although Jenny's slender, she has a little bit of curves in all the right places.

Me? Nothing. I'm so thin my breasts and ass are laughable at best, and it's not because I don't eat because trust me. I've gone hungry before, and you'll never see me turn down a meal or feign a weak appetite. I can put it away like a football player, and I'm not even the least bit ashamed of it. At barely five foot, though, I'm teeny tiny and still look like a pre-teen—no matter how much I eat.

My best friend and I are total opposites. She's outgoing whereas I'm quieter. I'm not exactly shy, but I don't have a desire to be the life of the party either. She's like the light, and I'm the dark. Seriously, I was born on All Hallow's Eve, and she was born on Jesus' birthday, a perfect little Christmas baby.

"Come on," Jenny grabs my hand and starts dragging me along with her, "let's go find some hot guys."

I roll my eyes. That's another difference between us. Jenny is boy crazy, and I couldn't care less about the opposite sex. I'm not a lesbian or anything, but I just don't have any experience with men.

Survival has kept me from getting into any serious

relationships. The most I've ever done is let a few boyfriends in high school kiss me, and I wasn't impressed with those slobbery attempts, so I've never been tempted to even try anything more.

So, yeah, I'm a twenty-year-old virgin. Pathetic, right?

Jenny drags me by a table filled with Halloween-themed cookies, cakes, and other confections, and my mouth begins to water.

I pull back on her hand to try to stay her. "Let's get some refreshments instead!" I yell to her over the pumping music.

She looks over her shoulder at me and rolls her eyes. "I swear, Eve, you're always freaking hungry. I don't know where you put it all."

I smirk at the obvious envy in her tone. Jenny is the stereotypical gym bunny, counting every calorie she eats to maintain her perfect physique.

"Don't hate," I grin at her smugly before reaching out to grab a miniature black cupcake covered with purple frosting.

I barely have time to pop the bite-sized confection in my mouth before Jenny is yanking on my hand again, pulling me through the crowd.

"Jenny, slow down!" I hiss at her, afraid I'm going to break my neck in these five-inch heels she insisted I wear tonight to make me not look like so much of a smurf. Her words—not mine. Plus, she claims they're just the perfect addition to the lacy black dress she dressed me up in.

I swear sometimes I think Jenny is my friend just because she wants a real-life doll to play dress up with. There's no greater joy for her than dressing me up in fancy clothes, doing my hair and makeup, and dragging me to shit like this with her.

And I go along with it because I love my best friend and want to make her happy.

Her eyes are scanning through all the masculine choices, and then she suddenly stops dead in her tracks.

"Oh. My. God." she breaths out.

"What?" my brows furrow at her melodramatic reaction.

"Check out Mr. Big and Scary," she breathes, and my eyes follow her line of sight and widen when they meet the object of her gaze.

A huge man in a black mask stands in a corner looking surly and brooding, towering over the other guests. The mask covers most of his face except his mouth. Think of the Don Juan mask Gerard Butler wore in *The Point of No Return* scene in that film adaptation of *The Phantom of the Opera*. That's what his mask reminds me of.

His hair is dark brown. It's stylishly disheveled, like

it's windblown and wild without looking messy. When he tilts his tumbler up and takes a sip of some liquid that's probably brandy or cognac or something else equally expensive, I watch his suit rustle as his muscles bunch with his movements like it's all the fabric can do to contain the beast within.

I don't know who the hell the guy is or what he does, but he exudes power and wealth. He's not wearing a costume like the other partygoers. No, he's wearing what I already know is a custom-tailored suit.

I don't need to be able to see all his features to see that he's gorgeous and dark and dangerous-looking. I've never seen a more perfect specimen of male masculinity, and my heart speeds up as my breath catches in my throat.

I've never reacted to a man this way before, and Jenny notices it if the sly, mischievous grin she gives me is any indication.

"I dare you to go over there and kiss him," she elbows me.

I laugh and push her back. "You're crazy! I'm not going to do that! I don't even know the guy."

"Exactly!" Jenny's eyes are excited. "You don't know him..." her voice sing-songs, "he's super smexy."

I roll my eyes. Only Jenny would make "smexy" a word in conversation.

Jenny ignores me and goes on, "You're twenty years

old today, and you've never had a decent kiss."

I glare at her, suddenly wishing I hadn't told her all the embarrassing details of my failed boyfriends.

Again she ignores me and keeps ticking off reasons I should follow her insane suggestion. "It's dark in here, and you'll never have to see him again. You can simply go lay one on the hot stranger and have a great memory for your birthday, and then we'll go eat cake and dance and party and everything will be perfect! You have nothing to lose and everything to gain!" she says happily.

I stare at her like she's sprouted another head.

Jenny is seriously out of her mind sometimes.

I'm laughing and shaking my head 'no' at her when she narrows her eyes and adds, "Plus, I'll give you a thousand dollars if you do it."

My laugh dies off as I nearly choke. "Whoa, wait. What?" I shake my head at her. "You can't be serious, right?"

Jenny's not laughing, though. She's looking at me challengingly with that I-want-to-get-you-in-trouble look that only a best friend can have.

"Dead serious. I'll give you a thousand bucks to walk over there and kiss that guy." She nods her head in his direction before that evil twinkle enters her eyes again. "And not just a quick peck on the lips. A real kiss. Like with some tongue."

I glance back over at Mr. Smexy. Jesus, did I just refer to him as Mr. Smexy in my head? I obviously need new friends. Jenny is rubbing off on me too much.

The man might be good-looking, but he's terrifying too. God, he could crush me with one hand.

And what the fuck will he think when some random girl comes up and kisses him out of the blue?

He'll probably have me arrested.

I'll embarrass the hell out of myself.

God, am I really considering this?

But, fuck, a thousand dollars? That'd give me a huge boost on paying my bills.

I look back over at Jenny. She's grinning at me impishly. She knows my struggle, and I think she halfway expects me to chicken out and not do it.

And that is what cements my decision.

I cross my arms and tell Jenny, "I want it in cash."

I see the surprise skitter across Jenny's face before she raises one delicate eyebrow and smiles like the Cheshire Cat, the glee practically oozing off her as she claps her hands together and laughs, "You got it, babe."

Before I lose my nerve, I take a deep breath, square my shoulders, and begin making my way over to the corner where Mr. Smexy skulks like some kind of standoffish canine.

I can almost feel Jenny's eyes boring a hole into my back, taking in the whole scene.

A thousand dollars. A thousand dollars, I chant in my head with each step I take.

As I get closer to him, he starts to notice my approach.

His head tips up, and his eyes laser in on me. The lighting is so dim where he's standing, it's hard to make out his features, but his eyes are golden and almost seem to glow like he's a vampire or wolf or something.

I swallow nervously and try to calm my racing heart.

A thousand dollars. A thousand dollars.

I just hope he doesn't bite me.

Lucian

My eyes are trained on a tiny form making its way in my direction, and they narrow as it gets closer.

It's dark in here, and lights flash out on the dance floor, but I've sequestered myself in this corner for a reason.

I don't want to be bothered.

In fact, the only reason I'm here is to meet with a business associate, and the fucker is late.

I'd much rather be back at my mansion. Alone. Secluded. The way I like to be.

I have no use for people beyond employing them.

Social settings aren't my scene and for good reason. The only reason I agreed to see my associate here is because he's only going to be in town for one night, and this is where he's going to be.

For some God forsaken reason.

And it's a masquerade-themed Halloween ball, so I can cover my scarred face. It's not that I particularly give a fuck what people think about it. I know that I'm still considered handsome, that maybe the cut that spans right side of my visage simply gives me that allure of danger that some women find so enticing.

But it's the questions I can't stand. The curiosity. The goddamned nosiness.

People don't know me. Nobody seeks me out. My demeanor is just menacing enough to off-put any curious eyes that glance my way.

So why in the hell does this little slip of a thing seem to be walking my way?

My eyes take in her long, dark tresses that flow down to her impossibly tiny waist. Milky white skin that almost seems to glow in the darkness.

Fuck, she's covered in lace. Her dress must be corseted if the way the two little globes of her breasts are pushed up is any indication. They're not large by any means, but just the sight of that little bit of modest cleavage has my blood roaring in my veins.

How long has it been since I've been with a woman? Since before the incident five years ago at least. I know I have enough money that I can still have plenty of women on my arm if I want.

That's not what I want, though. Shallow companions, fake smiles.

Since I can't have a connection, something real, I settle for nothing.

My hands work just fine.

But Christ Almighty, seeing a female approaching me after all this time has every nerve in my body pulled taut. I'm on edge and feel like I could blow at any moment.

My eyes drag back up her form to her head, most of which is covered with an elaborate peacock mask.

I can't make out her features through the dim lighting and all the ostentatious feathers that cover her face, but I see a flash of midnight blue before she's suddenly standing right in front of me. Her body isn't touching mine, but she's so close that I can feel her heat through our clothes, smell her scent. Violets and vanilla and something I can't identify.

Her head barely reaches my chest, and before I can ask her what she's doing, who she is, hell, anything, I hear her take a deep breath, and then she clumsily grabs my face and pulls it down to hers, pressing her lips firmly, if somewhat nervously, against mine.

I'm so stunned I don't react at first. But then my mind and body registers the feel of her tiny lips on mine. They're pressing softly against them, and then she takes my bottom lip in between her lips in an innocent, single-lip kiss. It's unpracticed, but god there's something so fucking hot about it, I feel a drop of precum bead the tip of my suddenly hard cock.

Hunger, hot and immediate, roars in my chest and bleeds through my veins.

I don't think. I just react, my hand reaching out to fist in her hair as I angle her head up to mine, deepening the kiss.

I suck on her bottom lip before my tongue forces her mouth to part, and she does so with a gasp of surprise.

I lick inside her mouth and taste her. Fucking hell, she tastes so goddamned sweet. Like pure sugar.

She whimpers, and that sound only spurs me on. I growl and mate my tongue with hers, desperate for more. More of her mouth. More of her.

I don't know who the fuck she is, but I know I'm not just turned into an animal because of five years of abstinence.

This is something more. Something primal. Like a wolf imprinting on its mate.

She tastes so fucking *right*. That might be a cliche, but fuck if I can help what I'm thinking and feeling.

Never, I mean, *never,* has a mere kiss affected me this way.

Just as I manage to set my glass of cognac down on a nearby table and am getting ready to pull her flush against my body, maybe throw her over my shoulder and stomp out of here caveman style and take her back to my lair and make her mine, she pulls away harshly, her little hands pressing hard against my chest.

We're both panting. I watch her little chest moving up and down as she gasps for breath. Her lips are ruby red and puffy and swollen from our kiss. I'm dying to see her eyes again, to demand who she is, where she came from, why the hell she planted her little lips on mine, but I never get a chance to ask any of that because she never looks back up at me.

Quick as a flash, she turns and runs away from me.

Panic explodes in my chest when I see her flying through the crowd.

Just as I start to take off after her, Adrian shows up and claps a heavy hand on my shoulder.

"Lucian, my man!" he greets me jovially.

I glance over at him distractedly, irritated that he took my attention off my little raven.

By the time I look back into the crowd, she's nowhere to be found. Rage and loss bubble up inside me to create a nauseating cocktail of emotions.

And I want to fucking murder someone.

CHAPTER 2

Eve

I can't decide whether to thank or murder Jenny.

I can't get that damn kiss out of my mind. It's just my luck that the best kiss of my life was to a total stranger on a dare.

God, I was so nervous. I don't even really know how to kiss properly, but boy did he.

He let me fumble around for a few seconds before he surprised the hell out of me by taking over.

And oh my god, *that's* what a kiss is supposed to be like. I suddenly know what romance writers are talking about when they write about passionate, toe-curling kisses. Honestly, after those bumbled efforts by high school boys, I'd half-believed the authors of those smutty novels were just full of shit.

But damn. Just damn. My toes curl and my entire body tingles just remembering the way he took charge, plundering my mouth with more skill than I could ever have imagined.

And the way he growled...like a hungry beast or something...like he wanted to devour me.

I felt the rumble resonate straight to my core. It both excited and frightened me.

When we finally broke apart for air, I panicked, my senses finally flooding back to me at what I was doing, and I ran on instinct, embarrassed as hell and ready to get out of there.

I'd returned to a gaping Jenny, who'd announced breathlessly, "Wow. That's the hottest shit I've ever seen."

But I'd ignored her and just grabbed her hand, yanking her out of the party with me.

I could not be confronted by that man.

No way.

Not after he'd just given me the highlight of my life, and I was nothing but a stupid little virgin.

Jenny had teased me mercilessly, but she'd gladly paid up and flitted happily back to college where she went on about her life like mine hadn't been altered forever.

That kiss.

That damn kiss.

It's ruined me for all other men.

I just know it.

It's the one I'll forever compare all others to. If I ever have any others, that is. I'm hesitant to ever let another man's lips touch mine and replace the memory of that perfect kiss.

It seems unlikely I'll have to worry about other men anyway now that I'm starting my new job for some reclusive rich guy who lives in a secluded, gated estate.

I stumbled across the ad in the paper one day on my lunch break at the shitty diner I work at. The ad said the employer was seeking a live-in maid for light housekeeping duties.

I applied just for the hell of it, never really expecting to get a call back, but I was called and hired a day later.

I had an interview on the phone with an older woman who pronounced herself the head housekeeper like something out of the Victorian era. She asked me just a few rudimentary questions before deeming me acceptable for the position.

I couldn't believe my luck. How hard was it to clean? The pay was more than I made at the diner in a month, and I'd get to live in a guest room rent-free as part of my "room and board," as she'd called it.

The relief of not having to worry about bills makes my step lighter as I walk up the massive front porch to the huge wooden door.

This exterior of this place is freaking gorgeous, like a mini castle or something, complete with ivy growing up the stone walls.

I know before the door opens that the interior will be just as impressive, and I'm not disappointed when an old man who's obviously a butler opens the door and I step into the marbled foyer.

The biggest, most beautiful chandelier I've ever seen in my life is hanging from the center of the massive ceiling right above the ornate, curving stairway.

My mouth falls open, and I immediately catch myself and close it.

No need for me to act like I've never seen wealth like this before in my life.

Even though I haven't.

I feel like a regular Disney princess who's stepped into a fairytale life. I can't believe I'm really going to get to live here, all in exchange for helping keep the place clean.

I give myself a little pinch to make sure I'm not dreaming, and I see the old man try to suppress a smile when he catches me.

My face heats, but I just smile at him and introduce myself.

"Hi, I'm Eve Carter, the new maid."

"Jenkins," he introduces himself with a nod. "Yes, Mrs. Monroe has been expecting you. Right this way please."

I follow him down several hallways, trying to pay attention to the many twists and turns, but I already know I'm going to end up getting hopelessly lost in this labyrinthian home.

I'm horrible with directions.

We finally reach the head housekeeper's office. Who knew head housekeepers have an office? Jenkins deposits me into the care of kind, if somewhat stuffy, Mrs. Monroe, and then she begins giving me the run-down on how things work in this household.

Lucian

"Dammit," I mutter as I sit down at my desk only to realize that my coffee and paper are missing.

"Jenkins!"

My butler appears a mere second after I scream for him.

"Yes, sir?" His face shows no emotion at my outburst.

I imagine my entire staff is used to my volatile temperament by now. And it's only been more explosive and frequent since that goddamned masquerade ball.

"My paper," I growl, "it's missing, as is my coffee."

"Ah, I see, Sir. Yes, Mrs. Monroe has been training the new maid. She's still getting the hang of everything, sir."

I pinch the bridge of my nose. Ah, fuck. Yeah, I'd forgotten about the new hire.

My old maid had finally retired. About time too. She'd been with my family since before I was born.

I don't begrudge the woman her retirement. It's well-earned.

But I run a tight ship. I like things the way I like them.

I don't like change.

I'm not thrilled about the disruption to my household. I hate any hitch in my routine. I trust my head housekeeper's judgement when it comes to hiring the staff that will primarily be under her, but whoever this new hire is has fucked up my morning, and I'm going to be ill as hell for the rest of the day because of it.

I grind my teeth together before I growl out, "Send her in here with my shit immediately. I don't care what the fuck she's doing. Tell her to drop it so I can get my day started properly."

"Yes, sir." Jenkins doesn't bat an eye as he turns to do as I directed.

See? Now that's good help. Immediate obeisance. No drama. No disruptions.

I sit back in my chair and scowl around my library.

I have a dedicated office space, but more often than not, I conduct my business from in here. Call me sentimental, but this space is where my father conducted his business and my grandfather before that and my great grandfather before that.

This library is steeped in my family's history, and now that my family is no more, I suppose I want to carry on as many of its traditions as possible.

I drum my fingers on my desk in irritation as I watch for my paper and coffee.

Yeah, I'm an impatient bastard. I hate waiting for anything, but I'm on edge even more so than usual because without my morning routine to keep me busy, my thoughts wander.

Back to that night.

Back to that kiss.

Back to *her*.

Whoever the hell she is.

Fuck, I can still feel her little lips pressing against mine, still taste her, still hear her whimper. In all my thirty two years, I've never experienced anything like that goddamned kiss that continues to haunt me.

God knows I've jacked my cock and come boat-loads to memories of that kiss every night since then.

And I have so many unanswered questions.

Why she'd pressed her little lips against mine in the first place being among the top of them, though now it doesn't matter.

I've tortured myself about it so much I've come to realize that I don't really give a fuck why she did it.

I just want.

I want *her*.

I have so many regrets.

Like how I wish I'd pulled her into my arms so I could feel her little body pressed all up against mine. How I wish I'd captured her right then and there and drug her back here whether she wanted to come or not.

How I should have at least demanded her name, anything, anything to go on.

I've had the best private investigator money can buy scouring the city, but without being able to give him more than a shadowy description of a masked form, it's been fruitless.

She's just gone.

It's like she's an apparition my desperate, lonely mind conjured up. Fuck, maybe I did conjure her up.

Maybe my self-imposed solitude is finally making me go mad.

I look up as a girl bursts into my office, almost tripping over her own two feet as she enters.

The tray she's holding wobbles, and I frown in annoyance when I see some of the coffee spill over the cup, no doubt getting my paper wet.

"So sorry, Mr. Claymore, sir," a soft, distinctly feminine voice apologizes nervously as she makes her way over to my desk and sets the tray down on it.

I'm still frowning as I take in her appearance. Her hair is piled on top of her head in an unkempt updo I think women call a messy bun, several dark strands falling down to hug her neck and kiss her face.

My heart jumps into my throat for a minute when I notice how dark the strands are. They're black as a raven's wing, shiny and silky looking, and they call to mind long, lustrous locks falling over black lace and hidden around peacock-colored feathers.

I shake my head as if to clear the mental image from it. Millions of girls have dark hair. Every one I run into can't be equated to my little masked raven.

Besides, this girl might be as tiny as my mystery girl, but she's even shorter than she was.

When she raises her head and looks up at me, time stops.

Midnight blue.

I see a flash of it in my mind's eye before those eyes close and little arms yank my face down to press the softest lips I've ever felt against mine.

I realize I'm just staring at the girl when she shuffles on her feet and looks away from me nervously like she's afraid I'm about to yell at her.

My frown deepens, somehow unsettled at the thought that she's afraid of me.

"What's your name?" my voice comes out harsher than I intend it to.

She frowns at my tone but answers back, "Eve."

"Eve what?" I prompt her for her surname.

"Carter," she instantly supplies.

I nod at her and then look down at my paper, clearly dismissing her.

I'll have my PI look into her, see if her name was on the ball's guest list for that night. It's too much to hope, though, that the girl from that night would be dropped right into my lap like this.

I'm not going to get my hopes up.

Still, even if this girl isn't her—and she likely isn't—she's a pretty little thing, and I can't stop my masculine reaction to her beauty.

Somehow that makes me feel...guilty? Like I'm betraying my little raven.

Fuck, that's fucked up. I'm feeling loyal to some girl I don't even know—all because of one mystery kiss on

Halloween.

And dammit, this is crazy. This girl is *not* her. She can't be.

I'm broken from my tortured thoughts when I realize the girl still hasn't moved. I feel her curious stare on me, and I look up at her and quirk an eyebrow.

"What is it?" I ask her impatiently.

She hesitates, and I see her eyes flick over to the scar running down the length of the right side of my face.

I grin at her sardonically, and her face colors. "Glass," I tell her simply.

Her eyes widen before she asks me cautiously, "How?"

"From a fire implosion," I state matter-of-factly with no emotion.

"Oh," she whispers, obviously getting the hint that further questioning is off limits.

"I'd better get back to Mrs. Monroe," she says breathlessly, and I watch her little chest move up and down with the words. She's completely covered in a black long-sleeved shirt and a pair of jeans, both of which only accentuate how slender she is. Her clothing isn't revealing at all, but something about her is so sensual and sexy, I feel myself lengthening and hardening in my pants.

I ball my fists underneath my desk, suddenly angered at this girl for making me feel this way.

"Eve?" I call her name sharply as she turns to leave. "I expect my paper and coffee to be waiting for me on my desk at seven sharp from now on."

Her eyes flash at the demeaning note to my voice, and I feel a prick of conscience at speaking to her in that tone.

She just purses her little lips and nods, and then I watch her exit, my conflicted thoughts and reaction to her still troubling me.

CHAPTER 3

Eve

My new employer is the grouchiest, growliest man I've ever had the misfortune to meet.

He sits behind his desk and glowers at me every time he sees me.

Sometimes I see his fists ball on his desk like the sight of me angers him.

Geez, am I really *that* annoying?

Lucian Claymore. That's what Mrs. Monroe told me his name is.

Fitting. His name is a play on Lucifer, God's most beautiful angel.

The embodiment of sin and evil.

Just like Lucian himself.

The man is hot.

No, I mean, he's seriously hot. As hot as the guy from the masquerade ball, but I know there's no way in hell my grumpy new boss is that guy simply because I can't imagine this man ever leaving this house.

Mrs. Monroe told me he rarely goes out, except for business, and a fun Halloween party hardly qualifies as business.

Still, he's tall and broad just like Mr. Smexy was. Yes, Jenny's nickname stuck. I still refer to my faceless, nameless kiss as Mr. Smexy.

Anyway, Lucian has stylishly disheveled hair just like Mr. Smexy did, except that when the light hits his dark locks just right, there's a glint of chestnut in it.

That scar on his face only adds to his appeal. It makes him look lethal, dangerous, like a warrior with battle scars.

The man exudes sexual prowess, and I can't help imaging what it would be like to have his big body on top of mine.

My heart thumps in my chest at the thought—in both exhilaration and fear. I'd be no match for a man like him. Not an inexperienced virgin like me.

I'm sure he's used to real women with amazing bodies like Jenny—not ones who still look like little girls like me.

Women with experience who know how to please a man—not fumbling virgins who've never even seen a man naked in real life.

And what am I thinking anyway? I don't want him. If I ever want anyone, it would be the mysterious man from the masquerade.

I'm so lost in my thoughts that when I round the curving staircase going up, I smack right into the subject of my thoughts as he's descending.

Like the walking hazard I am, I lose my footing and start to go tumbling down the stairs to break my limbs. My eyes snap shut in dread, and my entire body instinctively tenses to brace for the fall, but it never comes.

Instead, I'm hauled against something hard and held fast with a band of steel around my waist.

I open my eyes, and two golden orbs are glowing down at me.

Lucian is clutching me tightly to him, so tightly that I can feel every outline of his body where it touches mine.

And I might be a virgin, but I feel something very large and very hard jutting out from the area between his legs, and I know it's his erection.

My face colors, and I feel an answering throb between my thighs.

The air between us is thick with tension as he stares

down at me intensely, and then I see his head looming closer to mine.

I panic. It's insane, I know. Lucian is easily the most attractive man I've ever meet—Mr. Smexy aside since I didn't really meet him. Lucian is so hot, I should want him to kiss me.

But the memories of my kiss with the masked stranger have me wriggling against Lucian, trying to free myself from his arms before his lips can touch mine and erase away the masked man's kiss.

I realize my reasoning is skewed, but that's how it feels—like if I let another man kiss me I'll lose the memory of that amazing kiss, that another pair of lips will wipe the memory of his away, and I'm not ready to part with it yet.

Especially with someone like my employer, someone who could never really want *me*.

At my wiggling, Lucian sucks in a breath, and then I feel him press that hard part of himself roughly against me. He bites back a groan like he can't help himself, and then he growls out at me, "Stop!"

His harsh command stills me, and I stare up at his clenched jaw, watching as he takes two deep inhales before he finally pulls me up onto the top stair with him and then releases me.

He takes a step back and runs a hand through his

hair while he glowers at me like my presence is irksome to him.

My cheeks flame even more, but I square my shoulders and muster up as much dignity as I can. "I'm sorry. I didn't mean to run into you, Mr. Claymore."

He doesn't say a word. His lips merely thin, and his nostrils flare before he turns on his heel and walks past me, continuing on down the stairs.

Like I'm not even worthy of a response. I feel my own irritation rise.

He might be gorgeous as sin, but the man is surly as hell and has no manners.

Whatever. I stare after him for just a moment before I spin on my own heels and head off to complete the tasks Mrs. Monroe gave me.

Lucian

Damn it, I was just rude as hell to Eve. But fuck if the feel of her in my arms didn't have my cock instantly hard, her tiny body pressed up against mine supercharging me like I'd been plugged into a live outlet.

That scent. Violets and vanilla. It tantalized my senses and took me back to that night. Peacock feathers, midnight blue eyes gleaming like sapphires against creamy skin.

I'd wanted another taste, just to see if she tasted as sweet as I remembered.

But when she'd started struggling against me, I'd been brought back to a harsh reality.

Eve isn't my little raven. My PI has already gotten back to me. He checked the guest list for that night.

There was no Eve Carter on the guest list.

Disappointment had flooded me even though I hadn't really expected her to be her.

Had I?

Maybe I'd dared to hope.

But it doesn't matter now.

Eve's not her.

She's just a siren sent to tempt me to madness. A vision with deep blue eyes and raven-colored hair. Like my own fantasy made flesh.

Fitting that her name is Eve like the original temptress. Her hair is down today. It's long and black as sin, almost shining blue under the lighting from the chandelier. I wonder how many times I could wrap my fist around it.

I feel even more blood flow down to my swollen cock, and I grit my teeth in frustration before I change direction and head to my bedroom.

There's no way in hell I'm going to be able to focus

on anything in this state, and I'm too wound up to simply will my aching dick to go down.

Besides, the fucker doesn't listen anyway lately. He has a mind of his own.

I don't even take the time to undress completely and get into the shower. I'm too wound up.

I barely make it to my bathroom before I have my aching flesh in my hand, stroking it roughly up and down as I remember the taste of those lips, her heady smell, sapphires glittering up at me for just a moment underneath a peacock mask.

Unbidden, my thoughts turn to Eve, how delicious it felt to feel her tiny little body pressed against me, the silky texture of her hair, the pink rosebuds of her lips.

Fuuck.

I open my eyes, and there she is. Eve's mouth is a perfect little "o" as she watches me in the mirror. I must not have shut the bathroom door all the way. She probably came into my room on some chore from Mrs. Monroe and didn't realize I was in here.

I'll bet she knocked on my bedroom door, but I didn't hear her because I was in here, too consumed with lust to think straight.

I find that I don't give a flying fuck about any of it.

She hasn't realized I've noticed her yet. Her eyes are glued to my cock like she's never seen one before in her entire life.

Fuck, if that doesn't make me even harder.

A jet of precum shoots from my tip, but my strokes never slow as I stare at her in the mirror, my eyes skating over her form, from the gentle swell of her breasts to the tiny curve of her waist and the subtle flare of her hips, all completely covered in long sleeves and jeans again, but my imagination is vivid. I can almost see through her clothes with X-ray vision.

I can just imagine the dusty rose buds of her nipples, the pink flesh of her pussy.

She licks her lips and then bites down on the bottom one, and that's what does it.

"Fuck!" I groan as I feel my release thunder through me. It tears from my balls before jetting up my stalk and out of my swollen, bulbous head in violent, uncontrollable spurts as I come harder than I've ever come in my goddamned life.

Eve's eyes widen as she watches me ejaculate, and that makes me come even harder, spend shooting from the head of my cock in thick, sticky ropes as I imagine her lips around my swollen length.

Her eyes finally move up to catch mine, and when she realizes I've been watching her in the mirror, her creamy skin pinkens.

I can't help thinking her whole body probably flushes that delightful shade of pink when she orgasms.

Before I get a chance to say anything, she turns and flees.

And I can't help being reminded of my masked raven who'd done the same thing, her black hair fanning out behind her in just the same way as she ran.

CHAPTER 4

Eve

Hours later my cheeks are still burning at the memory of what I witnessed Lucian doing.

The way the muscles in his arms flexed as he stroked himself to release. The sight of the white jets of fluid shooting from his swollen erection like a party popper.

The deep growling, raspy noise that rumbled up from his chest when it happened.

And good lord, the sheer size of what his hand flew up and down. It makes sense he would be well-endowed. He's big all over, but sweet baby Jesus.

He was long and thick, and I can't imagine how he

could fit that inside any woman, much less one as tiny as me.

Still, that didn't stop a pulse from throbbing in between my legs like my body wanted to try.

My body is just stupid, though. It doesn't know any better. It's never had sex before, and I don't know why it thinks it could accommodate something of that girth and length.

Why it doesn't recognize that something like that could wreck it.

I'm sitting in Jenny's dorm now listening to her prattle on about everything that's happened since she's been back at college.

Fortunately, my best friend is so wrapped up in her chattering that she hasn't noticed my flushed countenance.

I came here just to get away from Lucian and his space for a night. I need some space to process after what I've just seen. Plus, I'm just so embarrassed to have been caught spying on him like that. How will I ever look him in the eye again?

But then I remember the intense hunger in his eyes, the lustful glint as he came while looking at *me*. God, am I the one who made his cock hard like that?

I blush anew just thinking about it.

Is it *me* he wants, or is it just that I'm the only young female in his presence? If he doesn't get out much, maybe it's just his body's natural response to any woman.

But even if he doesn't go out much, that's not to say he can't have a stream of women brought to him when he wants them. Lucian is very attractive. He could have his pick of any woman he wants.

And he always glowers at me like my very existence is a stain in the room.

I don't really think he likes me at all.

I chew on my bottom lip as I think. Jenny is still rambling on, oblivious to the fact that I'm not even paying attention to her.

Yeah, sometimes it's convenient that she's so self-absorbed.

I can't stop my mind from wandering to what it would be like to feel Lucian's lips on mine.

Although I feel like I'm betraying that amazing kiss for even thinking it, I think that Lucian might could kiss as good as Mr. Smexy.

Maybe.

I shake my head and focus in on Jenny, giving her an absentminded "uh-huh," when I find her looking at me to confirm I'm listening.

That must please her because she launches back into her monologue, and I retreat back into my thoughts.

It doesn't matter, though, I ultimately decide.

He's my boss, and I'm fairly certain he can't stand me, and I'm just going to have to go on and act like nothing happened and try my best to stay out of his way when I go back.

❦

Lucian

Where the fuck is she?

I pace back and forth in front of my library window, looking out over the driveway, waiting to see a taxi pull up carrying Eve back here.

Where she fucking belongs.

I can't fight this insane pull to her.

God knows I've tried. I've tried to stay away from her, but she's always there, silently doing her job in the background.

Cleaning like a damn maid.

Of course, I realize that's what I pay her for, but seeing such a beautiful creature of perfection reduced to such menial tasks as the hired help bothers me.

She should be draped in silk and dripping in jewels.

The way my body comes alive when I'm in her presence...the only other time I've ever felt this way was during that damn kiss on Halloween.

And despite the evidence pointing against my little

raven being Eve, I can't keep my suspicious from growing.

My *body* thinks Eve is the girl from the masquerade. My mind might logically tell me it's not, but I can't stop my senses from flooding every time Eve's in the same room as me.

She smells the same, her coloring is the same, her silhouette's the same.

The only thing off is her height, but I'm a dumb fuck for never considering that the girl at the masquerade could have been wearing heels.

All women wear heels to parties. Just a testament to how out of touch with things I am that I haven't considered it before now.

And her name not being on the guest list? Maybe she'd been with a friend, been someone's plus-one.

My jaw clenches at the uncomfortable thought that she'd been in attendance with another man.

But then, that can't be right because then she wouldn't have kissed me.

I roll up my shirtsleeves in frustration and continue to pace back and forth in front of the window like a caged lion.

I can't help it. I can't sit still wondering where she's at, who she's with, when she'll come back.

Who the fuck she really is.

I should have denoted a clause in her hiring

contract that she wasn't allowed to leave the premises without prior approval. I'm sure that would have been all sorts of illegal and she probably wouldn't have agreed to such a position, but fuck it.

I don't like not knowing things. I don't like not being in control.

I don't like waiting.

I gave Jenkins instructions to send her directly to me when she walks through that door.

I'm going to get my damn answers tonight.

Eve

My heart beats a frantic rhythm in my chest as I make my way up the stairs to Lucian's office. Jenkins promptly told me I'd been summoned straight to the master's office as soon as I walked in the door.

My belly is filled with an anxious ball of dread.

He's probably going to fire me for earlier. That has to be what this is about, right?

I square my shoulders when I'm just outside the door and muster up all the dignity I can. If anyone should be feeling ashamed, it's him—not me. If the little incident earlier was anyone's fault, it was his —not mine. I'd knocked on his door and when he didn't answer, I'd naturally assumed no one was inside. Like any normal, rational person would have.

I never imagined he was in his bathroom pumping his cock like a glorious beast in mating season.

My cheeks color again at the thought, but I shake it off.

He was the one who'd been masturbating and had actually continued going even when his maid had walked in on him.

I knock on his office door now and wait for his gruff "Enter" before I dare push the door open.

For just in case he's in another uncompromising position.

Fortunately, he's not. When I push open the heavy door, he's standing in front of the window.

I swallow nervously when I see his shirtsleeves rolled up and the top buttons of his white dress shirt unbuttoned. His hair is mussed like he's been running his fingers through it, but somehow it still looks stylish even in its disheveled state.

The man is still gorgeous.

Everything about him radiates powerful masculinity.

And that masculinity is currently primed and pissed.

"Close the door," he barks, and I jump.

I hesitate a moment, but at the flash in his eyes, I immediately move to do as he says.

"Where the fuck have you been?" he bites out at me.

I bristle at both his question and his tone. He might be my boss, but I don't know what gives him the right to think he can speak to me this way.

"Respectfully, Mr. Claymore," I can't help the dripping hint of sarcasm that enters my voice, "I don't have to report everywhere I go to you. I'm your maid. Not your slave."

A muscle in his jaw ticks at my words, and I know I've only angered him further, though exactly why he's so angered is beyond me. I completed all my tasks for the day before I left, and surely this isn't all about the incident earlier...

He's quiet for a moment before he nods his head tightly, conceding my point, I guess.

"About earlier..." he begins, and I stand there mortified that he's *actually* going to bring it up.

My face instantly colors and I panic, interrupting him with the first thing that pops into my head, even though it's a lie, "It's okay. It's nothing I haven't seen before."

His eyes take on a stormy look, and I rush to add. "Not to say that I've seen you before. You know, doing, um, *that*." God, I sound like such a bumbling idiot.

"And I am so sorry to have walked in on you doing, um, you know, but I *did* knock," I add for good measure, "and you didn't answer, so..." I trail off myself when he takes a measured step toward me.

I feel like I should step back, but somehow I'm frozen in time. I can hardly breathe, much less move, as he continues to walk toward me in slow, calculated steps.

He ignores the last half of everything I said, focusing only on the first part. "You've seen another man jerking his cock for you?"

His golden eyes are flashing with anger, and I suddenly regret my lie. I shake my head.

"So you're a little liar then?" he asks me with a raised eyebrow, although some of his anger seems to have been tempered.

I frown. "No, I—"

He hushes me with a finger over my lips.

My breath hitches at his touch, and all I can do is stare up at him.

His eyes darken as he takes in his big finger resting on my lips. He finally tears his eyes from my lips and brings them up to meet mine. "Tell me truthfully, my little liar. Have you or have you not seen a man's cock before?"

God, the way he bites out the word "cock" has me squirming uncomfortably under his gaze.

He smirks as if he already knows the answer and is reveling in my discomfort.

"Well?" he prompts me lazily, almost as if he's bored.

"No," I finally confess, and his eyes seem to light up with triumph.

"No," he confirms, his voice smooth velvet as his eyes trail over me from head to toe.

"And I'll bet no has ever touched you here." His voice is a low rasp as his hand skims over the underside of my breast, and I swear to God I can't breath. I feel dizzy. His touch has stolen my air and sent tingles rushing all through me.

"Or here," he whispers as his hand trails down over my waist and glides over my stomach down to where he cups me roughly between the legs, eliciting a gasp from me.

"I'll bet," he goes on huskily, "no one has even properly kissed you here," he taps that finger against my lips again, and something inside me snaps.

I remember that kiss on Halloween night—the one highlight of my life—and I'm suddenly angry at Lucian for making me feel like a silly little girl with no experience.

I might be a virgin, but I have one amazing kiss in my memories, and I'll be damned if a let this man take that from me.

"You're wrong," I whisper, and I watch his eyes harden with something I can't identify when I tell him, "My lips have been claimed, and I already know no one will ever be able to kiss me that way again."

Lucian makes a strangled sound of rage before he bites out, "Oh, yeah?"

"Yes," I hiss up at him challengingly. God, I don't know what I'm doing. Why I'm taunting him. I don't want Lucian to kiss me. I don't want to replace that perfect kiss with one from this beast of a man.

I can't want that.

Before I can even conjure up my next thought, Lucian growls deep in his throat—a growl that sounds so familiar—and then his lips crash down onto mine.

He kisses me skillfully, his tongue plunging into my mouth to find mine. His kiss is commanding, domineering, artful.

And I'm struck with a sense of deja vu so strong I almost collapse.

His lips, his tongue. The way he growls into my mouth and I feel the rumble all the way to my soul.

It's all too familiar.

I've been kissed like this before.

Jesus Christ.

Lucian is Mr. Smexy.

CHAPTER 5

Lucian

Fuck. I knew it. Deep down, I fucking *knew* it.

Eve is my little raven.

The taste of pure fucking sugar. The heady scent of violets and vanilla. Her tentative, unpracticed tongue, so innocent and pure and goddamned sweet it makes my chest ache.

She flew right into my cage.

"You!" she gasps out when she finally manages to tear herself from me.

Her midnight blue eyes are wide with shock and recognition, and then fear and embarrassment shutter through them before she turns and begins to run.

I'm on her in a flash, slapping my hands on either side of her just as she reaches the closed door.

I press my body flush against her back, my arms caging her in and keeping her from opening the door.

"Oh, no you don't," I breathe down at her. "You're not running from me again, my little raven."

I feel her body trembling underneath me, and I pull back just enough to turn her around to face me. Her pulse is thundering in her neck, and I stare at it, transfixed, still high on the adrenaline of both the chase and my discovery.

"How long have you known?" she asks me accusingly.

I don't answer her. Instead, I parry a question of my own back at her. "Who were you at the party with?"

Her eyes search mine before she answers softly, "My friend, Jenny."

I relax a bit, relieved she hadn't been there with another man, before I ask my next question, "Why did you do it?"

"It was a dare," she admits on a whisper as she looks up at me warily like she expects me to be angry about that or something.

And maybe I would have been at one time, but frankly, right now I don't really give a fuck why she did it. I don't really care that I was the butt end of some kind of dare between her and some silly friend of hers.

"I guess I should be glad you're brave then," I tell her, my voice coming out low and husky.

She just stares at me in disbelief.

"Tell me," I ask her as I slowly run my hand down her stomach and under the band of the top of her jeans, "when this masked man kissed you like no one else ever will again, did your little virgin pussy get wet?"

I dip my hand into her pants and under her panties, inching my fingers down to the hot heat between her legs. Her hands are digging into my arms, and her breaths are coming out in ragged little puffs right next to my ear.

So much blood rushes down to my engorged cock, I almost feel dizzy. I prop a hand against the door beside her head and then dip my fingers all the way between her legs to find her wet.

She's soaking fucking wet for me.

I can't stop the animalistic growl that tears up from my throat as I smash my lips back onto hers, kissing her with everything in me as I find her swollen clit and begin to flick my fingers over it.

She cries out into my mouth, and Jesus, I've never tasted anything as good as her cries. I want to eat them up.

Her arms circle around my neck and latch onto me, and I could practically roar in victory to feel her clinging to me like this.

She whimpers as I remove my hands from her pants, but I soothe her with soft licks on her lips as I work to pull her shirt up over her head. Then, I yank her pants down, leaving her in nothing but her little violet bra and panties.

My mouth waters at the sight. She's tiny perfection. I want to taste her all over, but just as I'm getting ready to lower my head to the swell of her breasts, she drops to her knees before me and looks up at me shyly.

My cock swells even more, straining toward her through the zipper of my pants as I read the intention on her face.

Fuck yes.

I'd be jealous as hell at the thought of her on her knees like this for someone else, but I already know she's never done it before by her own admission.

It'd be kind of hard to suck a cock if you've never even seen one before, and the thought that mine will be the first—*and only*—one in her mouth has a steady stream of precum leaking from my tip.

Her hands are shaking as she unzips me. She's moving too slowly, but I fight the urge to take over and free my aching rod.

I won't waste this gift she's giving me. I can be patient for her.

I groan when she finally releases me, and my heavy weight springs out and almost smacks her in the face.

She studies my cock with wide-eyed curiosity, running tentative fingers down its length in fascination.

I can't stop the rasping cry that bubbles up from my chest when she touches the precum at the tip wonderingly and then swirls it around the head.

I ball my hands into fists at my sides to keep myself from jamming my dick into her mouth and down her throat.

It's taking every ounce of restraint I have in me to hold still and let her explore me at her own pace.

"Jesus!' I hiss out when I feel her kiss the head of my cock, her tongue lightly licking the underside of it.

"Put it in your mouth," my order comes out hoarse, and I watch as she immediately obeys like she was just waiting for direction.

And fuck me, fuck me. The sensation of her hot, wet, little mouth sliding down onto my thick length and then her sucking as she glides her head slowly back up it is enough to make me see stars.

I finally do what I've wanted to do from the first moment I saw that long black hair of hers.

I wrap it around my fist three times and push her head further down onto my cock until I feel her gag.

I pull back once I trigger her gag reflex, knowing that it's too much and that if I don't stop now I'll blow my load down her creamy little throat.

I don't want to come until I've claimed her as my own.

She puts her mouth back on me again, though, and then looks up at me with those eyes, and I almost fucking lose it.

"Fuck, Eve," I groan and pull myself from her mouth with a noisy pop before I yank her to her feet and pick her up in my arms.

I carry her over to the sofa and drop down to my knees before her, my mouth already salivating at the thought of tasting her.

I taste the tiny buds of her nipples first, thrilling at the way she gasps and arches against me, her hands flying to my head to hold me there as I suckle her while my hands caress every inch of her I can find.

She's so responsive, arching into my touch, gasping and whimpering like a hungry kitten.

When I finally make my way to the heaven between her thighs, I spread her wide and then just look at her glistening pink folds.

She blushes in that way virgins do and starts to close her legs, but I hold them open and growl out at her. "You're the most beautiful fucking thing I've ever seen, Eve. Never try to hide yourself from me. Do you understand me?"

My voice comes out harsher than I intend it to, but damn it. I can't help it. My own hands are shaking with my barely restrained lust. It's all I can do to keep from ejaculating all over the floor just at the sight of her perfect pussy.

The first lick is like coming home. I've never tasted anything so right in my entire life. She tastes like *mine*.

I lick and suck on her folds until she's squirming and pleading for me.

"Please," her dark hair is splayed out all around her on the couch as she thrashes her head side to side.

"Please what?' I prompt her, desperate to hear my name on her lips. She's never said it before. She's only ever addressed me formally as "Mr. Claymore," and I can't tamp down the sudden need to hear my name dripping from her lips.

She looks down at me in confusion.

"Who am I?" I ask her as I tease my tongue against her opening.

She bites her bottom lip, and I growl before I raise up and suck on that very lip, making her taste herself on my tongue.

"What's my name?" I whisper against her lips. "Who is your masked lover you've been saving yourself for?"

Her cheeks turn a charming shade of pink, but she doesn't deny my assumptions, and a thrill goes through me at the thought that memories of that kiss have been haunting her just like they have me.

"Lucian," she finally whispers, granting my wish, and a surge of victory soars through me before I return to between her legs and reward her by sucking gently yet insistently on her swollen clit.

"Oh god!" She cries out as she arches up into my face.

I hold her still as I push one, then two fingers into her, testing her tightness.

She's breathing heavily, her eyes wild as they meet mine.

"Sshh, it's okay baby," I soothe her before I latch back onto her clit and swirl my tongue around it while applying rhythmic suction, knowing exactly what she needs to tip over the edge.

I gently stroke my fingers in and out of her before I curl them upward and find that spongy spot inside her that I know will trigger her release.

"Lucian!" she screams my name and her fingers dig into my hair as I feel her pussy spasm around my fingers, tightening almost painfully around them.

Fucking hell, I almost come just imaging how that hole will feel strangling my cock.

In fact, I fist that throbbing part of myself and squeeze to stem the boiling I can already feel in my balls.

Eve is laying lax, half hanging off the couch with her legs still slung over my shoulders, and I gently move her legs off me before I tear my shirt from my body and pick her up.

I sit on the soft cushions and then position her above me with her legs straddling me.

My cock surges up to nudge against her dripping wet hole with a laser focus of its own.

Her eyes find mine, and I see a flicker of doubt and fear there.

I stroke her cheek and then lean in to kiss her lips.

"Do you know how long I've been searching for you? I couldn't get the thought of you out of my head. You and that kiss have had me going out of my goddamned mind for weeks now," I tell her.

I feel her melt against me, and I position my cock right underneath her as I continue to speak to her, coaxing her to relax with both my words and soft slides of my lips against hers.

"Been nutting every night to memories of that fucking kiss, baby."

She whimpers at my words and kisses me back, her tongue sliding into my mouth this time.

As she relaxes, she begins to slip down onto me until the head is in her.

"Lucian," she whispers my name, her voice tight at the foreign pressure she's no doubt feeling now.

I just kiss her lips again, fisting a handful of her hair. I'm too strung tight to speak. I can't think. My blood is roaring throughout my veins with the need to claim.

Every muscle in my body is pulled taut as I concentrate on sliding slowly into her, as I fight the urge to thrust roughly up and bury myself in her completely.

God, she's so fucking tight and tiny. It's like a vise is gripping me.

I grit my teeth as I feel my balls coiling up, already ready to shoot their load.

I finally reach her hymen, and then we sit there suspended in anticipation, breathing each other's breaths as our lips ghost together, barely touching.

I want to ask her if she's okay, but I can't form words. This moment is too monumental for words anyway.

A beat passes. Then another.

And then I can't take it any longer, and I thrust up while pulling her down hard onto me.

"Mine!" I can't help crying out in victory as I feel her hymen breaking for me before I slip completely into her wet heat.

Eve cries out in what I know is pain, her arms tightening around me as she clings to me desperately.

My balls are resting flush against her, and she squirms on me, trying to get comfortable, almost causing my eyes to roll back in my head.

I grit my teeth and ignore the instinct to move, though. Instead, I focus on soothing my mate.

And that's what she is. It might be archaic and primal, but she's mine.

For life.

I'm never letting her go.

I stroke my hands down her back and kiss her lips before trailing my kisses over her neck. I suck the smooth column of her throat, wanting to leave my marks on her delicate skin, wanting that evidence that she's been claimed there for all to see.

"You take me so good, baby," I encourage her as I test her, slowly gliding in and out of her a half an inch.

She tenses for a moment, but then she drops her head against my shoulder and moans a sound of pleasure.

I continue stroking in and out of her slowly, taking my cues from her body.

I only pick up the pace when her moans become more desperate and she pleads with me, "Lucian, please..."

She doesn't know quite what she needs or what she's begging for, but I do.

I know exactly what she needs, and I'm sure as hell going to give it to her.

I begin to push up into her hard and fast while bouncing her up and down on me.

Her cries of pleasure are echoing throughout the library, and I pump into her harder, spurred on by the sounds of her screams.

I want to hear her shatter in ecstasy.

I want to be the one to give her her first orgasm with a cock deep inside her. I want to satisfy her that way.

Her wetness is dripping down onto my balls, and the glide of her silky heat up and down my cock is bringing me closer and closer to climax.

I yank her head back to force her to look at me when I feel the first ripples of her pussy around me, knowing she's fixing to come. Her mouth is open in that little silent "o," and she's fucking beautiful like this, in the throes of passion, on the brink of orgasm.

Her skin is flushed, her eyes are frantic, she's biting her lip and throwing her head back and moaning. Moaning for me.

Sweet Jesus.

"Oh fuck, yeah, baby. Look at me. Look at me," I command her. Her dark blue eyes find mine desperately. "Look at me when you come all over my cock."

My balls are churning, and I know I can't hold off any longer. I grit my teeth and find her clit with my thumb, rubbing it in circles, one, two, three times.

Her eyes go wild, and then she screams my name as she convulses around me.

I continue to slam into her, and then I feel my balls boiling over. I roar out my own release as the hot rush of my seed tears up my cock, the head swelling and then popping as I violently explode deep inside her.

Her pussy jerks around me in tight, pulsing spasms that suck my jizz from my dick, milking more and more from me, each pulse of her pussy causing an answering spurt to rise up within me until I've come so much I wonder if I'll ever be able to come again.

I come so much it overflows out of her pussy and drips down onto my balls, turning our sexes into a filthy, sticky mess.

The thought only makes me begin to harden inside her again, and I tighten my arms around her, holding her flush against my chest, relishing the feel of her breasts and stomach pressed against me.

"Lucian?" she finally whispers against my neck.

"What, baby?" I ask her as I run my hands possessively over her, trying to commit every bit of her body to memory. God, she's fucking beautiful, my woman.

"Where do we go from here?" she asks me uncertainly.

I know what she's asking. Jesus, how could she think I could ever want anything but this—anything but *her*—now?

"You're not going anywhere," I growl at her, and that elicits the tiniest of smiles from her.

She hides her face in my neck, but then I tilt her chin back up to make her look at me, "You're going to stay right here with me where you belong, my little raven."

She laughs, a sound that's music to my ears and then agrees, "Okay then, Mr. Smexy."

I raise an eyebrow at her humorously. "Mr. who?"

A blush overtakes her cheeks, but she holds my gaze as she grins at me. "It's kind of a long story."

"Mmm," I nuzzle my nose against her neck, deeply breathing in her violet and vanilla scent. "I've got time. The rest of our lives, in fact."

I look up into her sapphire eyes and decide that her eyes are the shade of blue that is now my favorite color.

Eve's midnight, sapphire blue.

EPILOGUE

One Year Later

Eve

My wedding ring is a sapphire—not a diamond. I wore a peacock-colored dress and violet undergarments. Nothing about our small wedding was traditional, but then again nothing about the way Lucian and I met was traditional either.

It was perfect for us.

My heart rate ticks up a notch as I make my way through the swarm of costumes and masked faces.

It's Halloween, my birthday, the anniversary of our first kiss, the day we met.

Our daughter, Jenna, is at home with Mrs. Monroe who loves nothing more than to play nursemaid to our precious baby.

We named her Jenna as a tribute to both my best friend, Jenny, and Lucian's mother, Anna. Turns out Lucian got the scar on his face from trying to save his family from a fire at their lake house. His mother, father, and brother all perished in the incident that had been caused by a freak gas leak.

He'd been bitter after the accident, naturally. That's why he'd become so reclusive.

Until he met me, that is.

It still humbles me to see how happy my husband is now. How willing he is to venture back out into the world so long as he has me by his side.

I'm not his maid anymore, of course. Ever since that fateful night when we discovered who each other was he hasn't let me lift a finger in the house. He stated that watching me clean had never set well with him anyway.

He didn't care that I told him I didn't mind cleaning and that I'd worked worse jobs to survive.

He'd just frowned and made me promise that from then on out I'd only do something I enjoyed.

So while he runs his business empire, I cook.

Seriously, I love food, so that's what I decided to do with my life.

I come up with new recipes and have a vlog that does surprisingly well. I've even published some cookbooks, but since Lucian and I don't need the money—he makes more than enough for both of us—all of the proceeds go to feeding the hungry.

Not only do I love what I do, but it makes me feel good about myself to know that I'm helping others.

Anyway, we named our daughter Jenna to honor both my friend, without whom we'd never have met, and Lucian's mother, without whom he wouldn't even be here.

I take another step and feel a prickle run up the back of my neck. I can sense that he's close.

I spin around and look through the sea of faces, but I still don't see him.

Suddenly, an arm snakes around my middle and pulls me back against a hard, broad chest. I gasp and then relax against him. I'd know his touch anywhere now.

He pulls me into a dark corner of the room before he whispers in my ear, "Up for a dare?"

He presses a kiss against the sensitive flesh right behind my ear, and I tilt my head to the side to grant him greater access before I answer back breathlessly, "Always."

I feel his smile against my skin as he says, "I dare you to kiss me."

I smile before I turn to look up at the masked face behind me. Amber eyes glow down at me in a mixture of adoration and lust. He's wearing the same black mask he was wearing that night a year ago, and I feel a shiver of anticipation rush up my spine.

My husband is still the hottest man I've ever seen.

Instead of pressing my lips to his, I reach up and slip the mask from his face before I do likewise to my own.

"No, *I* dare *you* to kiss *me*," I tell him.

His eyes gleam predatorily as he smirks at the challenge. "What's the wager?"

I cock my head and pretend to consider. "I'm not sure. What do you want?"

He grins wolfishly. "A little raven."

My breath catches in my throat as his lips descend upon mine, stealing my breath away just like he did a year ago.

His eyes are hooded when he finally pulls back just enough to look down into my eyes.

"You were right, you know," I tell him.

He cocks a brow at me with a grin, obviously pleased to hear me admitting he was right about something. "About what?"

"I am a little liar. Someone was able to kiss me that way again."

His grin turns cocky as he gets my reference and then pulls me flush against him.

"How about I try to do it again?" his lips move against mine with the question, and then he claims my mouth again.

In yet another perfect, soul-shattering kiss.

"Happy birthday, my little raven," he growls against my ear, and I sigh in total contentment.

Happy birthday and happy Halloween to me indeed.

THE END

Connect with Emma!

Visit Emma's website to get a FREE book you can't get anywhere else: www.authoremmabray.com.